Illustrated by
Mia Lloyd

Written by
Kristina Rowlands

The **Monster Zoo** is a very popular place for people to visit.

All sorts of Monsters live there.
**Big ones, small ones, scary Monsters
and kind, shy ones also.**

Felix is a **Fossil Monster**.
He lives at the zoo with his parents
and little sister **Freya**.

They also share their enclosure with their **uncle
Fabio**. He is a very old and wise Fossil Monster.

Felix's best friend is **Gaspar**.

He is a **Ghost Monster**.

Gaspar changes colour depending on how he is feeling.

If he is happy he turns **pink** and sort of fluffy and if he is angry he turns **completely black**, as dark as the night itself.

Gaspar and Felix get to see each other every day as they attend **Monster School** together.

They enjoy their lessons there and love playtime when they get to explore outdoors.

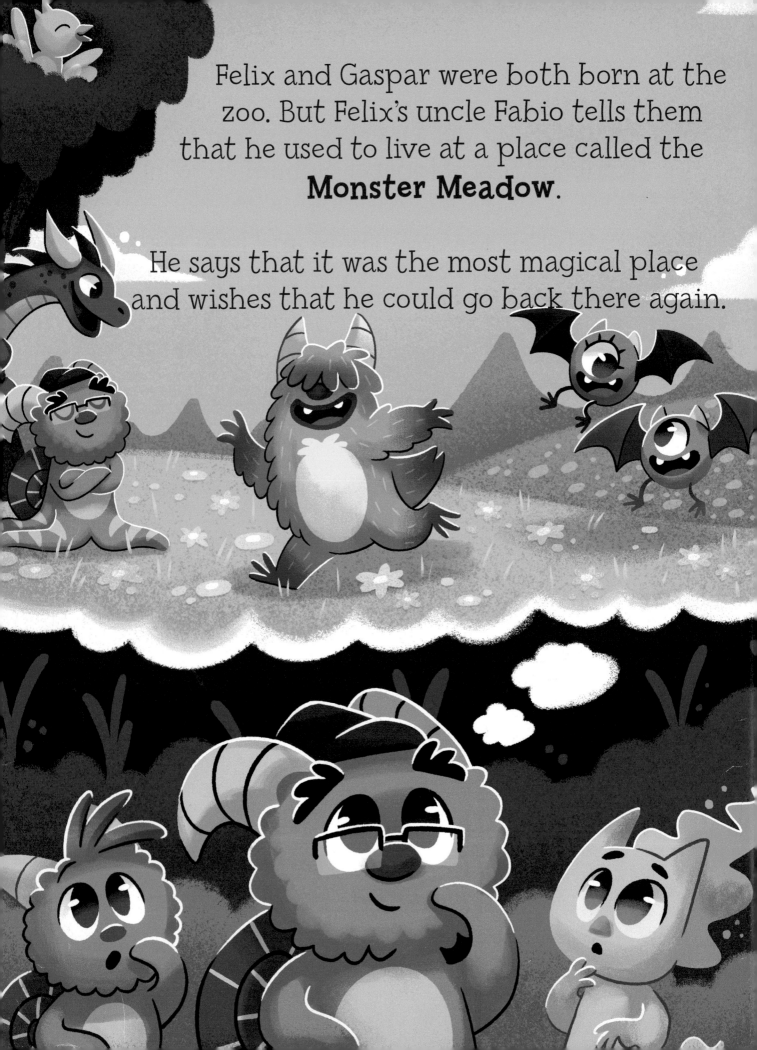

Felix and Gaspar were both born at the zoo. But Felix's uncle Fabio tells them that he used to live at a place called the **Monster Meadow**.

He says that it was the most magical place and wishes that he could go back there again.

Felix's parents say that the Monster Meadow does not exist anymore because all of the Monsters that used to live there have been chased out.

But Fabio tells Freya and Felix wonderful stories every night about the adventures that he used to have at the Monster Meadow and **his eyes light up in a special way at the memories**.

Gaspar has got a Granny who lives
with his family in their enclosure.

Her name is **Gracie**.

She also remembers the Monster Meadow with
great fondness and **her only wish** is to be able to
go back there again before she is too old.

All of the Monsters are being kept *prisoner*
inside the high walls of the zoo,
locked in their enclosures.
Only a few times a year are they allowed out
to have a **big Monster party** on the green
common in the middle of the zoo.

There is **music** and **dancing**
as well as **paddling pools**
and **ice cream** on offer.

Gaspar and Felix have started to talk a bit more about **how they can find out some more facts** about the Monster Meadow.

But whenever they try to ask their parents about it they always answer that they are all being well looked after at the zoo.

But Fabio and Gracie often sit together on the fun days, drinking their **Monster Coffee** and talking with great joy about the good old days.

They sometimes **draw maps** in the sand while remembering all of their adventures. They both believe that the Monster Meadow still exists somewhere.

Gaspar has had a bit of a difficult time at school lately. **Samar** who is a **Skunk Monster** and a bit of a bully has been teasing him. He has been saying that he believes that Gaspar fancies Maria, the Musical Monster.

Poor Gaspar can't help but change his colour and goes bright red, **as he gets really embarrassed** and everyone laughs at him, including Maria!

Felix has tried to help Gaspar by asking Samar to stop being so mean, but Samar then sprayed a **strong smelling liquid** all over Felix so that he stank for the rest of the afternoon and nobody could stand being next to him...

Freya has **also been feeling sad** lately as she had decided that she wanted to study hard to become a **doctor** or a **nurse**.

But then she realised that **there is no point** since there are no jobs available for the monsters after they have completed their studies at the Monster School as all the jobs are being done by humans.

Freya asks Felix if they can figure out how to **find their way** to the Monster Meadow.

They agree to make a plan together with Gaspar and over the next few weeks they collect a lot of information and begin to make a plan for their escape.

Felix explains to Freya that he does not think that it would be safe for her to come along.

"Me and Gaspar can both run faster and hide quicker," he says while giving her a reassuring hug.
"Besides, we need you here so that **you can be our messenger and look after the adults.**"

"I suppose so," Freya agrees quietly.

They all decide that Felix and Gaspar will make their escape during the big summer party when everyone is distracted.

They have carefully packed all of the information along with some warm clothes, snacks and drinks. They all say to each other

"We are best friends every day, we trust each other in every way.'

As dusk begins to settle over the park,
Gaspar and Felix sneak away to the far exit.
Gaspar changes his colour to a dark grey
and Felix can hide in his shadow.

Felix uses one of the Fossil bones on his tentacles
as a key and opens the gate as planned.

They have done it, they are finally free!

They reach the train station and sneak on to the night train leaving town.

They watch the stations carefully as they travel along and **manage to jump off at the right stop.**

A friendly troll has a deserted tree house at the end of this town.

The key is hidden under the mat just as described in one of Gracie's stories.

They will be safe there for a while.

On the second day they leave the tree house and set off through the deep forest.
They walk for hours trying to find the right way.

They need to be extra careful as the staff at the Monster Zoo have noticed that they are missing and there is a search warrant out for them to be captured and brought back to the zoo as soon as possible.

Late in the afternoon they begin to realise that they are lost. Feeling hungry and cold they start to argue with each other about which way to go.

In the distance they can see **some search lights** and decide to hide. They settle down for the night under a big pile of leaves.

The next morning after having rubbed the sleep out of their eyes they decide to walk in the complete opposite direction.

After a while the trees get thinner and they can see an opening to an industrial estate where there is an **old abandoned bakery shop**.
Felix can again open the door using his Fossil bones.

Inside the Bakery they find a freezer with some bread they can defrost and eat.

They decide to send a message to Freya to let her know that they are safe.
They receive a reply back from their parents. It says;
"No matter where you are, you are always in our hearts; A family's love never departs."

Just then there is a scratching sound at the door
and they both freeze with fright...
Before they know it a big brown bear is standing
tall in front of them growling loudly!

"Two little juicy monsters," he says in a dark
voice... **"You will be perfect for my lunch!"**

"Noo, **please don't eat us**!"
Felix and Gaspar shout in chorus.

But the bear is starving and in no mood to listen.
"My fossil bones will ruin your teeth and hurt your
stomach!" Felix shouts in a panic.

"I am a ghost!" Gaspar adds. "I will haunt you and
your family forever if you hurt us."
He changes his colour to a ghostly white
while shouting "**Boooo!**"

"Please don't hurt me," whimpers the bear,
curling up into a small ball.

"We will let you go if you agree to help us," Felix says quickly.

The bear whose name is **Benny** agrees.

He knows the way across the fields like the back of his paw. He can walk quickly with Felix and Gaspar travelling along on his back.

As they reach the big river in the afternoon they set up a campfire to make some tea.
All of a sudden they can see a beautiful unicorn watching them from a distance.
Benny knows its name.

"**Zuri!**" he calls
"come and say hello to my new friends!"
Zuri belongs to the Lava family; they used to live alongside the Monsters in the Monster Meadow.

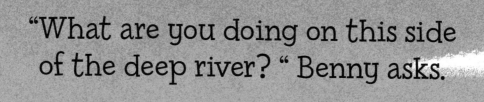

"What are you doing on this side
of the deep river? " Benny asks.

"I was looking for food," Zuri explains and then sits
down to tell Gaspar and Felix about it all.

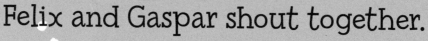

"The Monster Meadow still exists!" Zuri says,
"But it has moved to a new secret location,
I can take you there if you like?"

"Yes please!"
Felix and Gaspar shout together.

Benny says goodbye and Felix and Gaspar
jump on to Zuri's back.

**There is a special light shining bright
from Zuri's horn, showing them the way.**

As they land in the Monster Meadow
they are very tired but happy.

It is indeed the most magical place!

The next morning , an academic monster named **Aimer** comes forward and offers to help them. **They start a campaign to free all of the monsters from the Monster Zoo.**

They gain a big following and a new law is written for the Monsters and Unicorns to be able to live in peace and be free. **It is a big victory!**

A colourful aeroplane transfers all of the freed monsters from the Monster Zoo to the Monster Meadow within the next few weeks.

But the **Skunk Monsters** and some of the other big monsters choose to stay at the zoo, they love nothing more than being able to **scare and entertain** the public with all of their tricks.

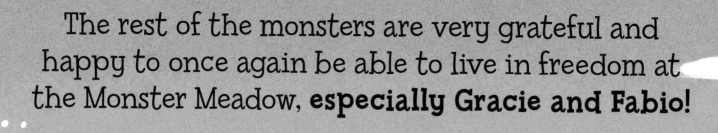

The rest of the monsters are very grateful and happy to once again be able to live in freedom at the Monster Meadow, **especially Gracie and Fabio!**

They celebrate with a picnic in the Meadow.

As Felix, Gaspar and Freya fly their kites high up in the blue sky, they all sing a new song together.

"Always believe that your dreams can come true, Always believe in yourself and the things that you can do!"